*For Frank: without him it wouldn't be as it is. E.T.*
*For Clément and Arthur, and all the blue stones*
*they'll be collecting throughout their lives. A-G. B*

*min*edition

*North American edition published 2019 by Michael Neugebauer Publishing Ltd. Hong Kong*

*Text copyright © 2011 Anne-Gaëlle Balpe*
*Illustrations copyright © 2011 Eve Tharlet*
*Rights arranged with "minedition" Rights and Licensing AG, Zurich, Switzerland.*

*Michael Neugebauer Publishing Ltd.,*
*Unit 28, 5/F, Metro Centre, Phase 2, No.21 Lam Hing Street, Kowloon Bay, Kowloon, Hong Kong*
*Phone: +852 2807 1711, e-mail: info@minedition.com*
*This book was printed in August 2018 at L.Rex Ltd*
*3/F., Blue Box Factory Building, 25 Hing Wo Street, Tin Wan, Aberdeen, Hong Kong, China*
*Typesetting in Candara*
*Library of Congress Cataloging-in-Publication Data available upon request.*

*ISBN 978-988-8341-75-7*
*10 9 8 7 6 5 4 3 2 1*
*First Impression*

*For more information please visit our website: www.minedition.com*

# The Blue Pebble

Anne-Gaëlle Balpe

with pictures by Eve Tharlet

Translated by Kathryn Bishop

Oli held a blue pebble in his arms.
He had found it under a daisy and decided to keep it.
Oli had never seen a shade of blue quite like it before.
And it had a funny shape—it was not quite round or square.
Holding the pebble tightly, Oli started on his way.

In the forest he met a wild boar.

"What have you got there?" asked the huge animal.

"Look, it's a lovely blue pebble," said Oli.

"What's it for?"

"I don't know yet," said Oli, "but I'm sure I will use it for something one day."

"There's nothing you can do with a pebble like that!" laughed the boar. "It's a waste of time carrying it around. Throw it away and start collecting roots and acorns for winter."

Oli said nothing.
He kept walking, clutching his pebble tightly.

Then he spied a wolf, hiding behind a great oak tree.
"What's that you're carrying?" asked the wolf, curiously.
"A blue pebble," said Oli, showing him.
"What's it for?"
"I don't know yet," said Oli, "but I'm sure I will find a use
    for it one day."

"There's not much you can do with a pebble like that,"
said the wolf, baring his teeth. "Don't waste time carrying it
around. Throw it away and look for a good stone you can use
to sharpen a stick. You might need a sharp stick to defend
yourself in this forest."

Oli said nothing.
With the pebble firmly under his arm, he continued on.

In a clearing Oli saw three elves playing marbles.
"What have you got there?" they called out.
"A blue pebble," said Oli, and he showed it to them.
"Is it useful?"
"I don't know yet," said Oli, "but I'm sure
  I'll need it one of these days."

The elves giggled and said, "It's barely round!
You can't do anything with that! It's a waste of time
taking it with you. Throw it away and find some nice
round pebbles. Then you can play marbles with us."

Oli said nothing and went on his way.

After a while, Oli saw a girl sitting on a large rock, crying sadly.

"What's the matter?" asked Oli.

Without saying a word, the girl showed Oli her doll. The doll only had one eye. There was just a gap where the other one used to be.

"Everyone says I should throw it away," the girl sobbed.

From behind his back Oli produced his pebble. It was exactly the same size and color as the doll's missing eye.
"Try this," said Oli. It fitted perfectly.
At last the doll had both her beautiful eyes again.

"I knew I would find a use for that pebble one day," laughed Oli with delight.

He picked up a thread the doll had lost, put it in his pocket, and went on his way. He had a feeling it might come in handy someday.